MY FRIEND IS DIFFERENT, AND THAT'S OKAY!

Written By
Mona Liza Santos

Illustrated By
Maria Dmitrieva

My Friend is Different, and That's Okay!

Copyright © 2021 Mona Liza Santos

ISBN: 978-1-955560-15-3 (Paperback)
ISBN: 978-1-955560-16-0 (Hardcover)
ISBN: 978-1-955560-17-7 (E-book)
ISBN: 978-1-955560-18-4 (Audiobook)

Library of Congress Control Number: 2021911564

Illustrations by Maria Dmitrieva
Layout by Shazeb Khan

First printing edition 2021.

www.monalizasantos.com

We don't have to be alike to be friends.

We just have to care about each other.

DEDICATIONS

To my son, Michael Blade, who is fascinated of everything galaxy and space related, I hope this book teaches you that no matter how different we all are, or where we come from – the most important aspect we must learn is that we all are the same because we can learn to accept each other and love each other for who they are!

This book is also dedicated to those who are inspired to travel to Mars someday! Who knows? Maybe we could make a friend from a different planet or galaxy!

THIS BOOK BELONGS TO:

_____

I've always wondered what it was like to be close to a star.
We now have rocket ships that take us far!

We could be on Earth for breakfast and Mars for dinner.
The chance to explore makes each of us a winner!

My favorite planet to visit is Mars, without a doubt.
I love exploring the craters it has, inside and out!

It's also fun to watch the two moons in the sky.
I like to think they're playing a game of tag way up high!

I love how Mars comes with this rusty-dusty sand.

You can see it covering the entire land.

Each step with a boot creates a satisfying crunch.

If you walk all morning, you'll be ready for lunch!

The reason I love Mars is because of the friend I met there.

He doesn't quite look like me, but I don't even care.

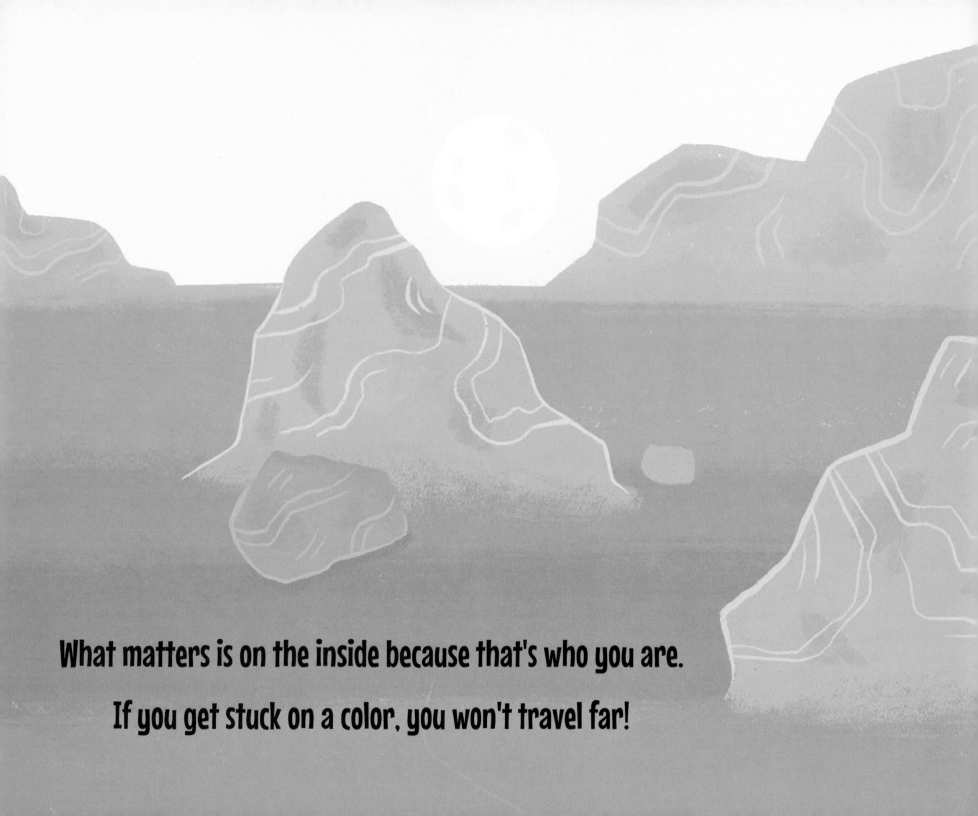

What matters is on the inside because that's who you are.

If you get stuck on a color, you won't travel far!

We run through the cities and laugh in the street.

We run until there's no energy left in our feet.

We run with spacesuits on so that we can breathe.

We run to find the secrets that are waiting beneath.

I love how Mars has different caves to explore.

You could find three today and tomorrow, four more!

Each one has a mystery that makes you think hard.

Does anyone on Earth have these chances in their backyard?

My friend and I each turn on our spacesuit light.

A Mars cave can get darker than the darkest night!

Then we carefully step around each rock on the ground.
Our breathing in the helmets is the only sound.

We'll see if we can find water or perhaps a remarkable rock.

One day, the scientists said that they'd found an old sock!

I always wonder if Mars was where life began.

I'm sure it started here with all this sand!

Once our exploring is done, before we say goodbye,

We watch Earth's blue dot twinkle in the sky.

I sometimes think about the people who live back there on Earth.

Do they know how much a new friendship is worth?

For too long, people thought that differences were bad.

Even the color of one's skin could make somebody mad.

Out in space, we know that we're all the same.

We represent humanity because that's our true name.

It's not about proving who is right or wrong.

When two friends come together, we both belong!

The rocket ship will blast off again with a fiery plume.

I can't wait to see how Jupiter's gases will bloom!

Whether my friend travels with me or stays at home,

We'll always be together in this universe we roam.

HOW WE CAN GO TO THE PLANET MARS SOMEDAY!

Mars is the fourth planet in our solar system and is half the size of Earth. Mars is also known as the "Red Planet" because of the reddish color of its surface. Its rocks and soil are rich in iron oxide, which give the planet its different red color. It is the coldest planet, also known as a "cold desert world."

Since it is within our solar system, Mars is an obvious priority for discovery, but there are many other reasons to explore this planet.

In many ways, Mars is Earth's brother. Seasons, polar ice caps, volcanoes, canyons, and weather are all present on it. Carbon dioxide, nitrogen, and argon make up the very thin atmosphere.

Have you ever imagined what life on Mars would be like? Humans' establishing a permanent residence on Mars is not an option. It's a necessity.

Let's have a look at how Mars can be an ideal planet for human life.

1. We can discover life on Mars

   If humans want to live for another million years, we will have to go where no one has been before, bravely. And there is no better option than Mars.

2. Elon Musk has creative ideas about Mars

   Scientists are studying how to live on Mars, and they believe it is possible. Elon Musk is excited about life on Mars, and he wants a million people to join him on the trip.

3. We must protect our planet and its people

   We all know Earth is the only home of humans. However, history has shown that living on this tiny blue dot in space is becoming difficult day by day.

Putting humans on many planets will guarantee our survival for thousands of years.

Elon Musk recently told astronomers, "Humans need to be a multiplanet species."

4. Planet Mars is similar to our Earth

There are many similarities between Mars and Earth. Both planets have seasons and similar day and night patterns. Since Mars has a day about the same length as Earth's, it is an ideal spot to live.

5. Mars has a lot of places to visit

The surface of Mars offers a few great opportunities for sightseeing. There would undoubtedly be areas that would become national parks if we were to colonize Mars fully.

6. There is evidence of the presence of water

There is confirmation of liquid, salty water underground on Mars, especially on hillsides. This is fantastic. If people go there in the future, they may discover more surprises.

7. Can we plant trees on Mars?

Yes, we can plant trees on Mars. We just need to make some changes in its atmosphere and soil to make it perfect for trees to grow.

8. How do you get to Mars?

Engineers are designing spacecraft and rockets that will bring us all to Mars one day. Are you ready to go to Mars? Then don't forget to bring food and water with you.

"Mars is there, waiting to be reached." — Buzz Aldrin

Mona Liza Santos, Author

Mona Liza Santos is the author of several children's books. She writes engaging rhyming stories about self-love and kindness and, most recently, age-appropriate spooky tales. Mona was inspired by her son and children everywhere to write, wishing to instill an early love of reading and to teach kids the importance of kindness and being true to oneself. Mona fell in love with writing as an escape and sees it as a way of leaving a legacy for her son they can both be proud of. When she is not writing, she enjoys spending time with her son, going to beaches, walking in parks, reading, and writing books. She has visited almost 60 countries and plans to see more in the future. Her main concern is ensuring that her son is healthy and happy and that she can continue to write books that leave a lasting impression on her readers. Stay up to date with her books at www.monalizasantos.com.

Maria Dmitrieva, Illustrator

Maria Dmitrieva is an illustrator of children's books. She lives in St. Petersburg, one of the most beautiful cities in Russia. All her life, she has wanted to do what she is doing now, and she is very happy to help book authors bring their ideas to life. Maria has illustrated other books and drawn postcards, and she started her career at a very early age with custom portraits. Her hobbies are reading books on psychology and watching movies.

Follow her on Instagram: marrr_shine

DESIGN YOUR ALIEN

Some Cool Facts About Mars

- One day on Mars lasts 24.6 hours. It is just a little longer than a day on Earth.
- One year on Mars is 687 Earth days. It is almost twice as long as one year on Earth.

- Several missions have visited Mars. One day soon, people will be able to go to Mars.

- Mars is a cold desert rocky world. It is half the size of Earth. Sometimes it's called the Red Planet. It's red because of rusty iron in the ground.

- Mars has two moons. Their names are Phobos and Deimos.
- Mars is the fourth planet from the Sun. That means Earth and Jupiter are Mars' neighboring planets.

Dear readers,

Hello there! First off, I am thankful for your support in reading my book - *My Friend is Different, and That's Okay!* If you believe this book would be a benefit and an inspiration to others, an hones review on Amazon or where you purchased this book from (Google Books, Barnes & Noble, Target, Walmart, etc.) would be greatly appreciated!

Your thoughts on my book would help me brainstorm other amazing ideas for my future books and of course, keep me motivated in writing inspirational, motivational, and enchanting stories like these. I hope this book inspires you to learn more about the planet Mars, because one day I'm sure people will b able to go to Mars if given the chance to! Wouldn't that be exciting? I have always been fascinated with our solar system and knowing that there's a possibility for people to step foot on Mars someday is just mind-blowing! Feel free to also share my books on your social media as well! 😊

I appreciate every one of your support and remember to stay focused on your dreams! Stay blessed! Thank you so much!

With much love and respect,

Mona Liza Santos

You can also check out my other books on Amazon by typing in my full name or visiting my website at
www.monalizasantos.com